WHITEOUT

by Kay Livorse
illustrated by Dave Kramer

HOUGHTON MIFFLIN

BOSTON

When Mary Alice woke up, she was startled by . . . silence. She heard no dogs barking, no traffic on the street. Where was the train whistle that usually woke her? Everything seemed so calm and quiet.

Mary Alice jumped up and looked out the window. Snow! Everywhere she looked. The whole world outside was white as . . . well, snow!

She ran into the next room to tell her brother Charlie the good news. She jumped on his bed to wake him up.

Mary Alice and Charlie raced downstairs. Mom and Robert were already making breakfast. Charlie headed for the door to the yard.

"Whoa!" said Robert. "Breakfast before play, sport."

Robert was their stepfather. Their real father had died when Charlie was five. Mom had married Robert last year. Mary Alice had warmed to Robert right away. Charlie was still getting used to having someone in his dad's place.

"Great," said Charlie with a frown. "Look who made it home last night."

"Did you have trouble on the roads, Robert?" Mary Alice asked.

Robert had been a player for the Cleveland Browns football team. Now he was a police officer. He often worked late into the night.

"Got a ride just in time!" said Robert. "With all this snow, the roads will be closed for days. Plows can barely keep up."

Mom held up her hand. "Listen! They're talking about the storm on the radio," she said.

"Six hours into the blizzard and no end in sight. Folks, we've got a whiteout here. A record snowfall for eastern Ohio! People are warned to stay— " The radio went dead. The lights went out too.

"Yippee! Power's out!" said Charlie. "Who needs lights in the day, anyway?"

"Got plenty of coal in the cellar, though," Robert added. "At least the house'll keep warm."

But right now Mary Alice and Charlie didn't really care about a warm house. They had snowmen on their minds. They gobbled up their eggs and ran to the door.

"Mom, can we go out and play now?" Charlie asked.

"Sure," said Mom, "but dress warmly. Hats *and* mittens."

Mary Alice and Charlie dashed out the back door into the white swirl of snow.

"Stay in the yard," called Robert.

"Yes, boss," Charlie replied. The door slammed behind him.

Mary Alice had never seen such deep snow. She and Charlie flopped around in the drifts. They tried to build a snowman. They laughed and threw snowballs. Then Charlie headed toward the toolshed. He started to climb up on one side.

"Hey!" shouted Mary Alice. "What are you doing up there?"

"Look at me! I'm Super—" yelled Charlie. Before he finished the word, he jumped. He held his arms out like a superhero. But instead of flying, he flopped. Right into a huge drift of snow.

"Owwww!!" Charlie screamed from under a white pile. Mary Alice couldn't see him.

"Charlie!" cried Mary Alice. She tried to run to him. But the deep snow made it hard.

"My leg!" moaned Charlie. Now Mary Alice could see her brother under the pile of snow. He was crying and holding his right leg.

Robert rushed out the back door. He'd heard Charlie's scream. He plowed through the snow towards Charlie's red snow hat.

"What's the deal there, sport?" he called to Charlie. Robert could barely get through the snow too. But he made it to Charlie before Mary Alice.

Charlie saw Robert coming. "I'll be all right," he said. "I don't need any help." He tried to stand. His leg hurt so much he almost passed out. He fell back into the snow.

Robert picked Charlie up and carried him into the house without a word. Mary Alice followed. She saw that Charlie was in too much pain to talk. She knew he didn't want to, anyway.

Robert took off Charlie's boots and gently felt his lower leg. Mary Alice could see that the limb was swollen. Tears filled Charlie's eyes.

Robert frowned. "Looks kind of like a broken leg there, sport," said Robert. "Some ice on it will keep it from swelling more."

"I'll get a pan and fill it with snow," said Mary Alice.

"Great idea," said Robert. "Snow will work fine."

Mom tried to call the doctor, but the phone was dead too. "What'll we do now?" she asked.

"Keep Charlie on ice," said Robert. "I'll walk
to the police station. There's a hospital on the
same street. I'll bet that street has been plowed.
I'll find a doctor or something . . ."

"But that's miles away!" said Mary Alice.
"How can you walk that far in this deep snow?"

Robert grinned and reached into the coat closet.

For a moment, Charlie forgot about his pain. "What are those things?" he asked.

"Snowshoes!" said Robert. "They let you walk in deep snow. Growing up in Vermont, I used my snowshoes all winter long."

They all watched Robert bundle up and strap on the snowshoes. Mary Alice thought he looked like he had tennis rackets on his feet.

"Be back with help in a jiff, sport," Robert said to Charlie. "Everything'll be okay." Then he disappeared into the blowing white storm.

Mary Alice kept getting more snow for Charlie's leg. Mom made peanut butter sandwiches for lunch. Charlie tried not to think about his leg.

"Do you think Robert can get someone to help?" Charlie asked.

"Yes," said Mary Alice. "I think Robert can do just about anything."

Mom smiled and started to read them a story to pass the time.

Mom was getting to the good part. Then, all of a sudden, they heard a rumbling noise outside. It was a snowplow, followed by an ambulance! Out of the plow jumped Robert.

Robert walked into the house with the ambulance driver. Mary Alice saw Charlie crack a small smile.

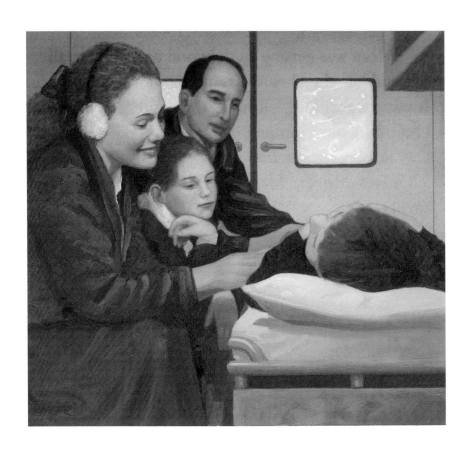

They all rode in the ambulance with Charlie.
Mary Alice could see Charlie staring at Robert.

"You're not so bad after all," Charlie
finally spoke up. "For a guy from Vermont."

Robert grinned and said, "Well, Charlie, I
guess once you get to know me, I'm not all bad."

And the whole family smiled as the
ambulance cut through the white walls of snow.